HAMM AND MEGS

GARY BATTERSHELL

Published by Water Dragon Publishing
waterdragonpublishing.com

ISBN 978-1-962538-26-8 (Trade Paperback)

FIRST EDITION

10 9 8 7 6 5 4 3 2 1

AUTHOR'S NOTE

I didn't set out to write a sci-fi rom-com, but that's how Hamm and Megs wanted it.

For my wife Emily,
who also hooked up with an alien life form.

HAMM AND MEGS

IMPERIAL DECREE REGARDING COLONIZATION

Be it known that henceforth all bans on the colonization of primitive alien worlds are lifted. It is expected that the processes of subjugation and occupation will be carried out with honor and restraint. The leaders of such efforts may rest assured that their actions will ultimately benefit those natives coming under the benevolent protection of the Benetine Dynasty and prevent their otherwise inevitable fall to the brutal and odious Tharg Dominion.

Issued by His Sublime Majesty, Harlo XV, Emperor of the Volian Empire, in the one hundred and twelfth year of His reign.

Megan shifted the straps of her backpack for the thousandth time and wondered yet again why she had agreed to do this. Was keeping in the good graces of her roommates, Gretchen and Cindy, worth a ten-mile hike up a mountain? The answer seemed to be "yes." Megan had never liked hiking, or mountains, or fresh air, or exercise of any kind, but she had never had friends before, and they both liked all of that.

Gretchen topped a rise and sat down on a convenient limestone outcrop. Cindy sat beside her and looked back down the trail at Megan.

"How you doin', Megs?" Cindy drawled. She was from Alabama, so she could drawl with the best of them. "You look like a landed fish suckin' for air."

"I'm okay," Megan lied, "for an overweight Jewish girl in the friggin' wilderness."

Cindy let out one of her magnolias-and-mint-julip laughs and Gretchen joined in with her Bronx cackle.

"I'd be mad," Megan said, "but I know you guys are laughing with me, not at me."

"But, honey chile, y'all ain't laughin'."

Megan made it to the rock where she hauled out like a walrus mounting an ice floe. The other girls had already stripped off their backpacks, and Megan was happy to do the same.

"I think it's past time for lunch," Gretchen announced, extracting a granola bar and a bag of peanuts from her pack.

"You sure it's safe to eat that?" Megan asked.

"What'cha mean?" Gretchen asked around a mouthful of peanuts.

"You might gain an ounce, and then Tony'd have to find some other stick-girl."

Gretchen grinned and tossed in another handful of peanuts. "If I wasn't so blonde and beautiful, I might take exception to that. And, for the record, Tony loves me for my engaging personality and inquiring mind."

"And the blowjobs," Cindy added helpfully.

"Well," Gretchen conceded, "there are those."

Megan fished a moon pie and a canteen out of her pack. She took a big bite of the former and small sip from the latter. "I've drunk most of this," Megan said. "Cindy, are you sure the lake water's gonna be drinkable?"

"We'll drop some purification tabs in just to be sure, but the guidebook said that the water this high up was as pure as any you get out of a tap."

"Don't tell me that," Gretchen said, shuddering slightly, "my dad works for NYC Water."

Cindy said, "Look, y'all. I wouldn't have dragged your asses up here for spring break unless I had thoroughly researched everything. It'll be great. We're gonna camp, smoke some weed, and just generally commune with nature."

"We could have done all that in Palm Springs," Megan said.

"Or Cancun," Gretchen added dreamily.

Megan rolled her eyes. "Like we could afford Cancun."

"I can dream, can't I?" Gretchen said.

"I've never found dreaming very useful," Megan said. "My people learned a long time ago to temper our expectations."

"Oh, Megs, here it is again," Gretchen said, "who're you gonna whine about this time, the Egyptians, the Babylonians, or the Germans?"

"Your people never suffered like mine," Megan countered.

"Which people? Swedes? New Yorkers? Art history majors?"

"Y'all quit it," Cindy said. "accordin' to the map, the lake's just over the next ridge, and it's gonna be dark soon. We need to get there in time to set up camp."

"You're right," Gretchen said. Turning to Megan she added, "I'm sorry, Princess. You know I was just playing."

•   •   •

They reached the lake as the sun was starting to set, its dying rays reflecting from snowcapped peaks far to the east. Behind and beside them, massive redwoods and stately lodgepole pines ran all the way down to the water and surrounded a greensward perfect for a campsite.

"That's the bluest water I ever saw," Megan declared. "This whole place is too gorgeous to be real."

"It's pretty, all right," Gretchen agreed. She grinned at Cindy. "I guess you aren't such a bad vacation planner after all."

"Can we go swimming?" Megan asked.

"You can stick your toe in and see how you feel about it then," Cindy said. "This water comes off a glacier. My guess is you'll just want to look at it."

Megan sat down on the grass and took off her hiking boots. She walked gingerly to the water's edge and squatted to dabble her fingers.

"I think I could swim in it, but maybe not for long, and not with night coming on."

The lake was on forest service land, and only primitive camping was allowed. Cindy found a level spot a few yards from the water, and it took only minutes for the girls to erect their pop-up tents.

"We should gather wood for a fire," Gretchen said.

Cindy agreed, and, while Megan found rocks for a fire ring and set up the propane camp stove, her friends took off for the woods.

While Gretchen and Cindy foraged for firewood, Megan heated water for tea and dehydrated stew. By the time darkness settled in, the girls had finished their dinner and were comfortably seated around the fire under the light of a nearly full moon. Cindy and Gretchen sat facing the lake with their backs resting against their packs. Megan sat across from them in the collapsible camp chair she had insisted on bringing, with the explanation: "If you two get your tiny asses wet, it's no big deal, but mine's plus-size."

"We'll cook a real breakfast in the morning," Cindy said. "I'm gonna get up early and catch us some rainbows."

Gretchen seemed skeptical. "Fish for breakfast?"

"You've never heard of kippers?" Cindy said. "I'll bet Queen Liz has 'em all the time."

"Well," Megan said, "if it's good enough for the royals, I'm game."

"What the hell," Gretchen agreed, "spring break should be a time of experimentation, risk-taking, debauchery."

"Not much to debauch with up in here," Megan said.

"We got weed." Cindy dangled a loaded zip-lock bag.

"Are you kidding?" Gretchen said. "Weed's not dangerous anymore. Doctors prescribe it to grandmas." She reached into her backpack and took out a bottle. "This, on the other hand, will fork you up."

Megan looked interested. "What you got?"

Gretchen handed her the bottle.

"Wild Turkey?"

"A hundred proof."

"This might kick off a respectable debauch," Megan said cautiously.

The lake shore lit up like a giant flashbulb had gone off, and a sound like a sonic boom caused Megan to drop the bottle and cover her ears.

Cindy and Gretchen jumped to their feet and Megan tried to, but tipped her chair over instead. By the time she was on her feet all was dark and quiet again.

"It was a fireball out over the lake!" Cindy said. "It fell in the water!"

"Yeah," Gretchen said, "I saw it, too."

"I was looking the other way," Megan wailed.

"Must have been a meteor," Cindy said.

Gretchen was skeptical. "Why would a meteor explode in the air?"

"You think it was a plane?" Cindy asked.

Gretchen shook her head. "How could it be? We never saw any lights or heard a motor."

For the next few minutes, the girls posited a number of explanations ranging from the supernatural to the scientific. They pretty much ruled out ball lightning and the beginning of the rapture but were still strongly considering space debris from a falling satellite when Cindy suddenly pointed across the lake.

"What's that, ya'll?"

Megan and Gretchen looked out over the gently rippling water. Indistinct under the moonlight, something was moving smoothly and steadily shoreward.

"It's big." Gretchen said.

"I think it's a man," Megan said, "on a boogie board?"

The object continued its approach.

Gretchen said, "That's not a boogie board, but it's a man, a real nice one."

The approaching stranger appeared to be standing in a silent-running, motorized boat that looked like half a clam shell. He was tall and muscular and dressed in a form-fitting coverall that glowed slightly in the moonlight. His hair was long and pale, and his right leg appeared to be encased in some sort of brace that extended from lower thigh to mid-calf. Beside and slightly behind him stood what appeared to be a child with an enormous head and skin the color of wheat dough.

"That's a grey," Megan said in raspy whisper.

"A what?" Cindy rasped back.

"The little one, it's a grey alien. Haven't you ever seen a movie? And the big one must be a Nordic."

"What?"

"They're aliens that look like Vikings. Travis Walton met one."

"Travis who?"

"Oh my God, Cindy, *Fire in the Sky* Travis Walton? You don't know ... you're hopeless."

"He's like a male version of *The Birth of Venus.*" Gretchen gushed.

"The what of what?" Megan asked.

"You know, Boticelli's painting with the naked bitch riding the sea shell."

"That's insulting to women," Megan said.

"Okay, that promiscuous slut of a goddess riding the sea shell."

"That's better."

A few yards from shore the strange vessel's bow grounded and its rider — clumsily lifting his braced leg over the side and wincing as it took his full weight — stepped out into the shallow water. He looked back at his small companion who, after a moment's hesitation, slid over the side. The little being was no more than three feet tall, so the water came to its waist.

"Should we run?" Megan whispered.

"From that?" Cindy whispered back. "He makes Leonardo DiCaprio look ugly."

"I don't mean to intrude," the man said, as he haltingly waded shoreward, "but after I crashed into the lake the first thing I saw was your fire."

"You aren't intruding one little bit," Cindy said. "We're glad to help. You say you crashed an airplane into the lake?"

The man waded ashore and smiled as he offered his hand. Cindy shook hands with him while bending to the side slightly to get a better look at his diminutive companion.

"Not an airplane," the man said, "my craft was a reconnaissance vehicle powered by ionic energy. Your species has not yet developed anything approximating its capabilities."

Megan's mouth flew open. "Are you talking about a flying saucer?"

The man laughed slightly. "A quaint description. No, my vessel was triangular in shape."

"And what's that thing you rode in on?" Megan asked.

"That is an emergency transport, a lifeboat, if you will. I'm afraid that it's all that's left, aside from myself and Oshi."

At the sound of his name, the grey waved a three-fingered hand.

Gretchen eyed the man wolfishly. "You must be traumatized, crashing and all. Why don't you and your friend sit down by the fire and we'll get you some tea. By the way, I'm Gretchen, and these two are Cindy and Megs."

"Thank you. I would like to rest a bit. My leg's giving me some pain."

"Did you hurt it in the crash?" Cindy asked.

"Yes. I did a quick scan of the injury before abandoning my sinking ship and applied this brace. I'm afraid the femur is fractured, and the kneecap needs repair. The brace will help with healing, but I really need medical attention. By the way, my name is Hamm, and Oshi is my service drone."

Gretchen took Hamm's arm and led him to the fire. She insisted that he rest against her backpack and accept some tea.

"Ah, Earl Grey?"

"We don't have that." Gretchen said.

"It's all right. I was just messin' with you, as you say; I'm from outer space, you see, and Captain Picard was always drinking Earl Grey on *Star Trek*. Really, I'd prefer water."

Megan said, "For an alien, you sure know a lot about us, and your English is better than ours."

Gretchen handed Hamm a bottle of water and sat down beside him. He thanked her and said, "We've been studying your species for five thousand Earth years. We know a lot."

Gretchen placed her hand on Hamm's arm and stroked the slick material of his coverall. "You want to tell us about what happened?"

Oshi had been hanging back. Now he moved fully into the firelight and Megan took a good look at him. Hairless; big head; pasty skin; eyes like giant black almonds; no clothes; and no visible genitals.

Megan's eyes went almost as wide as Oshi's: "You're real! "You're actually an alien!"

"Yes," Hamm said, "and you're actually an aborigine."

"What are we supposed to do with you?" Megan asked. "Take you to our leader, maybe?"

"If we wanted that, don't you think we'd have met your leader already? Besides, your planet doesn't have a leader, you've got dozens."

Gretchen looked reproachfully at Megan. "You need to calm down, girl."

"You really do, sugar," Cindy agreed. "Hamm here's not a mean alien, he's a nice one, and I'll bet his little friend's nice, too."

"We need to help this man, not give him grief," Gretchen added.

"Well excuse me for being afraid of aliens," Megan said indignantly. "What if he wants to probe us or something."

"I don't believe I'll respond to that suggestive remark," Cindy said imperiously.

Megan looked to Gretchen for support, but the prospect of alien probing hadn't seemed to frighten her either.

"I can assure you," Hamm said, "that I mean you no harm. I have to ask something of you that may sound harrowing. The fact is that I was on a mission to save your race from destruction when my craft was attacked. With my injury, completing my mission now will depend upon you. I cannot force you to help me, but if you don't, the human race is doomed."

"No pressure there," Megan said.

Hamm gently detached Gretchen's hand from his arm and stood up. He limped to Megan and put his hands on her shoulders. "I appreciate your honesty, and I don't blame you for questioning my motives. But rest assured, if I did mean harm to this world or to your species, that harm would never befall a native as enchanting as yourself."

Megan saw expressions of shock and confusion on the faces of her beautiful roommates.

"Okay," Megan said, "maybe you ought to sit down and tell us about how we can help save the human race."

•   •   •

"That was horrible," Cindy said as she toweled off and slipped into her panties, jeans, and shirt. "That water's as cold as a penguin's pecker."

"You crackers are just pansies," Gretchen said. She had finished her morning ablutions earlier and was making oatmeal and toast on the camp stove. "That's what comes from having just two seasons, summer and almost-summer."

"I'll thank you to eschew the ethnic slurs, please?" Cindy said with exaggerated affront.

"Well, eschew you," Gretchen replied.

Megan crawled out of her tent, stood up, and stretched while she finished buttoning her shirt. "Yeah, Cindy, You don't seem to mind when she calls me 'Princess,' or 'Jewbaca.'"

"Well, of course not. That's funny."

"I never knew that bothered you, Megs," Gretchen said.

"It kind of does."

"Well, then I'm gonna be kind of ashamed of myself for doing it anyway. Soup's on."

Gretchen handed bowls to the other girls and spooned in the thin, lumpy stuff.

"Toast is ready, too," Gretchen said.

Each girl took one of the three slices of toast sitting on the four-slice camp toaster. They ate sitting cross-legged around the embers of the morning fire.

"Not too bad," Megan pronounced.

"Not too bad?" Cindy said. "Oliver Twist ate better than this."

"I thought you were going to catch us some trout, Cindy," Megan said.

"Hamm kept us up too late."

"Hey, where is Hamm?" Megan asked.

"Don't know," Gretchen said. "I was up before you guys and he was already gone."

"He should have slept in one of our tents instead of out here in the open." Cindy said.

"We offered," Gretchen said with a wan smile.

"Megan didn't," Cindy said with a malicious grin. "I'll bet he'd have slept in her tent, 'enchanting' as she is."

"Cut it out," Megan said, "that's embarrassing."

Gretchen rolled her eyes, "A guy that looks like a Greek god says that to you and you think it's embarrassing? Would winning the lottery be gauche?"

"He's an alien," Megan said.

Gretchen rolled her eyes. "You didn't believe that load of granola, did you?"

"He crashed a UFO into the lake, and he had a grey with him," Megan said. "Yeah, I believe it."

"That little sucka' was weird," Cindy said. "I've had boys give me the eye before, but not with eyes as big as hubcaps."

"I say it was some kind of a joke and we won't see him again," Gretchen said.

Cindy said, "You're just pissed because he didn't think you were enchanting."

"No," Gretchen replied, "that just makes me think he's nuts."

Megan finished her oatmeal and set her bowl aside. She stood up and pointed north toward mountains lower and closer than the big snowcapped ones to the east.

"It's that one," Megan said, "the peak in the middle. That's where Hamm said the bad aliens have their base. That's where we have to go."

"Because they shot down his UFO?" Gretchen said incredulously.

Megan turned to face her friends. Her expression was serious. "That's not all he said. Hamm said that his mission was to destroy the base before they could launch an assault on Earth. He said his ship was equipped with cloaking technology, but that the enemy, what did he call them?"

"Zeelons," Cindy said helpfully.

"Yeah, Hamm said the Zeelons must have developed new sensors that located him when he flew too close."

Cindy rolled her eyes. "You really believe that?"

"Don't you? You did last night."

Hamm emerged on his transport from out of the treeline. The small vessel glided silently just above the ground as easily as it had moved through water. Oshi stood to Hamm's rear holding a cord that served as a stringer for several trout.

Hamm glided up to the campsite and dismounted the transport, clumsily due to his leg brace. Oshi jumped lightly down from the hovering craft and proudly held out his laden stringer.

Hamm said, "Last night someone said something about trout for breakfast and I thought I'd go get some."

"Without a rod and reel, and on a bad leg?" Cindy said.

"Oshi is a drone of many talents," Hamm said, "fishing is one of them. As to my leg, the brace dulls the pain and promotes healing. As I told you last night, I'm not helpless, but I can't complete my mission now, not alone."

Oshi went to Megan and proffered the stringer.

"It wouldn't take long to cook these up," Megan said, taking the fish from the drone. "We had some oatmeal, but it was pitiful."

Hamm smiled softly at Megan. "We have time for that," he said, "but I'd like to reach the Zeelon base by midday."

Gretchen looked skeptical. "And start our mission of sabotage, I suppose?"

"Yes," Hamm said, "as I told you, it is unlikely, injured as I am, that I could successfully plant the explosive and escape."

"What if they catch us?" Cindy asked. "That'd be bad, wouldn't it?"

"Probably not. The Zeelons do not see natives as a threat."

"So, if they get us, it'll be catch-and-release?" Cindy asked.

"Probably."

"Wouldn't they worry we'd tell on them?" Gretchen asked.

"Alien visitors to worlds such as this, like the Zeelons or my people — the Etherians — rely on the ignorance and the inaction of the natives. On planets without knowledge of the cosmos and its plethora of intelligent races, few natives report alien encounters for fear of ridicule, and those that do are rarely able to convince enough of their fellows to make a difference. Killing or detaining natives is much more likely to lead to problems than releasing them."

"I can see that," Megan said.

"Of course," Hamm said, "your insight and intellect are as obvious as your beauty."

"Like your enchantingness," Gretchen added.

"I can see that you still have reservations," Hamm said. "If you'll accompany me to the Zeelon base, I'm sure I can convince you that what I am saying is absolutely true."

"I'll go," Megan said, putting her arm around Hamm's waist. He draped a brawny arm around her shoulders.

"Absolutely unbelievable," Gretchen mumbled.

"I assure you," Hamm said, "that what I have told you is true."

Gretchen shook her head as though to clear it. "No, I meant … never mind. I'm in for the trip, but maybe not the mission."

"Me, too," Cindy said.

Following their meal of grilled trout, Hamm boarded the transport and beckoned for the girls to follow suit.

"It will be a bit tight, but we can all fit," Hamm said.

The transport lacked seats, but there was plenty of standing room. Hamm allowed Gretchen and Cindy to board on their own, but extended a hand to Megan and pulled her up beside him. When Oshi, the last to board, was in place, he swung the craft about and glided north.

"How do you make this thing go," Megan asked. "I see a control panel, but you aren't touching anything."

Hamm tapped his forehead. "It's synchronized with my brain waves."

"You mean nobody else could drive it?"

"Not like this, but there are manual controls."

The craft automatically adjusted for changes in grade and avoided obstacles with easy precision. There was never a sense of tipping or shifting, even on inclines. When Megan attempted to extend her hand past the gunwale she met spongy, invisible resistance.

"That's our version of airbags," Hamm explained.

After about an hour, the transport stopped on a mesa overlooking a cliff face at the bottom of which was a large cave opening.

"That's an entrance to the Zeelon base," Hamm said.

Favoring his braced leg, Hamm climbed down from the transport, and, once on the ground, offered his arms to Megan. He swung her lightly down as his other passengers debarked on their own.

Hamm led the girls to the mesa's rim.

"That's pretty steep," Megan said. "Can we even get down there?"

"It's not as bad as it looks," Hamm said.

"And tell me again, why exactly do we need to go in there?"

"The Zeelons have almost finished their portal. When it is complete, countless thousands of them will come pouring through, armed with weapons for which the people of your world have no counter. In days they will establish planetary supremacy."

"And they'll enslave humans?"

"Not exactly."

"They'll just kill us all?" Gretchen posited.

"They are carnivorous," Hamm said. "They'll establish breeding farms here as they have done on other planets."

"Oh, that's disgustin'," Cindy drawled.

"We do it to cows," Gretchen observed.

"In any case," Hamm said, "you can see that they must be stopped."

"Why don't they just come in starships," Cindy asked, "like in the movies?"

"Star travel is neither cheap nor fast," Hamm explained. "Once the portal is operational, the Zeelons will be able to instantly transport soldiers and materiel to your world."

"Couldn't we just nuke 'em?" Cindy asked.

"Compared to the weapons the Zeelons will bring, your nuclear arsenals would be useless."

"Why do you care?" Gretchen asked. "Doesn't your species think humans are lower animals?"

"Certainly not," Hamm said, and looked at Megan. "Unlike the Zeelons, we respect other sentient beings. Earth natives have intelligence ... and other endearing qualities."

•   •   •

Hamm spent some time explaining in detail his exact plan. He finished by opening a compartment in the vessel's wall from which he extracted a tennis-ball sized, tan-colored orb which he handed to Gretchen.

"So this thing's full of antimatter?" she asked.

"Essentially," Hamm affirmed. "Most of the orb's interior is composed of ionic shielding, but there is sufficient antimatter inside it to destroy the Zeelon base."

"And we're supposed to plant this on the portal?"

"Correct. You will make your way to the cavern where the portal is under construction and leave the orb in its vicinity. When the Zeelons generate the wormhole allowing their forces to cross, the radiant and kinetic energy released will crack the shielding inside the orb, and — BOOM!"

"But there's no danger of us going boom, right?"

"No. Our intelligence indicates that the Zeelons are weeks away from finishing the portal."

"What if they find the orb in the meantime?" Megan asked.

"Hopefully, that won't happen. Once the orb is planted, it will morph into a shape, color, and texture that conforms with the surface on which it has been placed."

"But won't the base be heavily guarded?" Gretchen asked.

"This section of the base is not in use. An earthquake rendered it unstable."

"You mean it might fall down on us?" Gretchen said.

"Unlikely."

Gretchen did not look appeased.

"Also," Hamm added, "this is not yet a purely military installation. It's currently staffed mostly with scientists and technicians. And, as I said, if you are apprehended, it is likely that they would do no more than administer a memory nullifying drug and release you."

"That sounds scary," Cindy said.

"There would be no permanent harm," Hamm said. "Considering the consequences to your civilization if the portal were to be completed, I think you must agree that the risk is small."

"You gonna give us directions?" Gretchen asked. "I'd hate to get lost in there."

"I will, but I must return to my craft for that. From there, I can access data from our remote scans and relay it to you. You may start immediately. Once you enter the cave, the first mile is a straight chute with no diverging passages. After that, you'll need direction."

"I thought your ship was burned up," Cindy said.

"No, only disabled. It's sitting, sealed and ready, at the bottom of the lake. I just can't move it until it's repaired."

Hamm handed Gretchen what looked like a large, silver bracelet. "Put this on, please."

Gretchen did, and it shrank to fit her wrist.

Hamm said, "I can transmit detailed schematics of the base through this device. Unless they see it in use, the Zeelons will not recognize it as other than jewelry."

"Okay," Gretchen said doubtfully.

Hamm continued, "One of you will need to stay here, at the top of the cliff, to monitor and adjust the signal as I project it, Megan, I think."

"How do I do that?" Megan asked.

"It's simple. When I detect distortions caused by atmospheric or mineralogical effects, I will relay the need for a correction and you can strengthen or weaken the signal as necessary."

Hamm reached into the same recess from which he had extracted the orb and took out a device like a small laptop computer.

"This is a signal regulator," Hamm said and handed the device to Megan.

Megan watched as Hamm activated the screen and a pulsing line appeared against a gridwork background. The line, Hamm explained, represented the strength of the signal. Once he began to transmit, if the line sagged below or rose above a certain range on the grid, it was Megan's task to bring it back into position.

"That seems easy enough," Megan said, "I just push it up or down with my finger. But couldn't you just do that yourself? Then we could all go."

"No, my dear," Hamm said, "I need you here."

Gretchen looked doubtfully at the orb in her hand. "There's no chance this thing could go off prematurely, is there?"

"None," Hamm said, "the shielding only dissipates in the presence of the particular energy mix released by the portal."

Gretchen seemed unconvinced, but she dutifully buttoned the orb in her shirt pocket.

Hamm took what looked like two ordinary flashlights from the transport. He gave one to Gretchen and the other to Cindy. "I'd like to provide you with more sophisticated lighting devices, but the Zeelons cannot suspect you've had contact with Etherians."

"What if they find the orb on us?" Gretchen asked.

"See that they don't," Hamm said with a smile.

Hamm left Oshi with the girls and climbed aboard the transport. Megan watched him cross the mesa and drop below its far rim. She looked wistfully after Hamm for a moment, and then turned to her friends.

"Guess I'll be seeing you guys later," Megan said.

Gretchen and Cindy were alternating looking down the steep slope and at each other.

"I don't think I want to do this," Gretchen said.

"Me, either," Cindy agreed. "Gretchen, can you use that thing on your wrist to send a message to Hamm telling him we respectfully decline?"

"I can try," Gretchen said.

"Wait a minute!" Megan said. "I know it's scary, but we have to do it. If we don't, the Zeelons will eat us, and our friends, and our families, and everybody."

"How do we know that?" Cindy asked. "Have we even seen a Zeelon?"

Megan jabbed a finger at Oshi, who was watching their argument with apparent interest. "We've seen that. Are you still saying that's not an alien."

"Hell, I don't know," Gretchen said, "there were guys in my high school creepier than that."

"You're just afraid," Megan said.

"Then why don't you go?" Cindy challenged.

"Because Hamm gave me another job."

"I can do that," Cindy said. "I watched him show you how, and there's nothing to it."

"All right, I'll go," Megan said, handing the regulator to Cindy and relieving her of her flashlight.

"How about you, Brooklyn?" Megan asked. "Are you a coward, too?"

"No," Gretchen said resignedly, "I'll go if you will."

"Fine."

With that Megan went to the mesa's edge and began to gingerly pick her way down. Gretchen shrugged in Cindy's direction and followed Megan.

Cindy heard a commotion behind her and turned to see Oshi slapping his hands together and jumping around in a frenetic way that suggested either religious fervor or extreme agitation.

"What's wrong, little guy?" Cindy asked.

Oshi pointed over the edge of the mesa and shook his head.

"Well, we didn't want to go. Your boss made us."

Oshi began to chatter shrilly. Cindy could tell that he was speaking a language and not just jabbering, but she had no idea what he was saying.

After a while Oshi quieted and went to the edge of the mesa where he knelt, watching the two girls' progress. When they entered the cave, he shook his bulbous head and sighed.

●   ●   ●

When Hamm was directly over his submerged but completely intact ship he took the transport down, its protective energy field providing a barrier against the water. At his approach, an automated hatch irised open and the transport slipped into a docking bay. While the water drained and the atmosphere stabilized, Hamm removed and discarded his leg brace; then he lowered the energy field and hopped lightly down to the deck.

Hamm made his way to the control center and brought up the schematics of the Zeelon base collected by Etherian probes. A complex tapestry of lines and spaces appeared on his screen, the lines representing corridors and the spaces, chambers of various sizes. At the center of the screen was the largest space, the portal chamber. Hamm touched the screen and a white blip appeared that marked the position of his team of reluctant warriors on the way to their unwitting sacrifice.

Hamm suffered a twinge of guilt. His plan was working, but he had not expected to fall in love. When Gretchen and Cindy came within range of the incipient portal, its energy field would trigger the antimatter device to detonate. On her hilltop, Megan would be safe from vaporization, but Hamm strongly feared that the event might damage their emerging relationship.

He had never known a woman like Megan. She was so square, and dark, and substantial, so very different from the women of his race, all of whom were boringly similar to Megan's two friends. If Hamm had not devised a way to save Megan, he might have abandoned the plan altogether; better, perhaps, to suffer his father's disappointment than to be the author of his love's destruction.

Hamm enjoyed his royal life, but he had always known that it carried obligation. After the third failed attempt to destroy the portal, his father, King Soros of Etheria, had come under immense pressure from the Legislative Council. There had even been rumors of calling the Electors into session for the purpose of selecting a new king.

How Soros had raged. "I won't have it! My legacy will not be the destruction of the Tyronian Dynasty!"

Zeelon and Etheria were sister worlds, orbiting the same red dwarf star on tracks so close that at perihelion, each filled half the other's sky. The rivalry between them had always been vicious; if the Zeelons were allowed to complete their portal and bring this rich new world into the Empire before Etheria could accomplish it, there would no longer be any question as to which planet was superior. The Emperor's gratitude and esteem would be showered on Etheria's rival.

And so, the king had made an address to the Council in which he proposed to send his own son, the Crown Prince, to do what others had failed to accomplish.

King Soros had appeared confident that Hamm would succeed in his mission of saving Etheria from humiliation and impoverishment, but he had provided no plan of action. Hamm had gone to Etheria's best military minds for advice, but none was forthcoming.

Etheria was, of course, constructing its own portal for an invasion of Earth, but its project, tucked in a remote arm of the Zagros Mountains, was much further from completion than that of Zeelon. Thus far the Etherians had only been able to complete only a small version, totally inadequate to move the necessary soldiers and materiel. Hamm, by destroying Zeelon's incipient portal, would be buying Etheria the time it needed to finish its own.

When he teleported to Ethereia's Earth base, Hamm was sadly convinced that the only way to get the antimatter bomb near enough to the portal to achieve detonation would be to sacrifice his own life or that of his drone. The second way was better, but it was highly questionable whether Oshi could have accomplished the task. While the synthesoid drones were very handy and quite reliable under supervision, giving them complex work to perform independently was asking for trouble.

It was when he had almost reached his objective and likely doom that Hamm had noticed a native campfire, and a new plan had struck him with all the force and glory of a supernova: he would recruit natives to do his dirty work. When he explained to them the dire danger for their entire species, how could they resist, especially if he left out the part about dying in the ensuing explosion?

•   •   •

Gretchen's wrist grew warm under the bracelet. She glanced down and saw a floating projection of the Zeelon base's layout. A red line marked their route, and their current position was indicated by a pulsing white blip.

"Hamm's transmitting," Gretchen said.

She shone her light down the passage. Ten yards ahead a corridor branched off to the right.

"That's our first turn," Gretchen said.

They entered the corridor, and, after a brief examination of the stone wall, Gretchen said, "There's no way this is natural; it's too smooth. And that must be damage from the earthquake."

Gretchen referred to vertical cracks, some more than a yard wide, that pierced the wall at irregular intervals.

Megan passed her hand over the stone wall. "It's smooth all right, almost like somebody poked a hot needle through the mountain."

"Or a laser," Gretchen posited.

"No wonder Dr. McCoy was so nervous all the time," Megan said, "aliens are friggin' scary."

"Hamm said they won't hurt us, even if they catch us?"

"I trust Hamm," Megan said, "but what if they find that thingamajig in your pocket. They'll know what we're up to."

"It's shielded. Hamm said there's no way they have instruments that will detect that it's a bomb."

"What if they probe us?"

"You think a lot about probing, don't you, Princess?"

•　　　•　　　•

Cindy was feeling a little guilty about chickening out and sending Megan in her place. She started slightly when the screen in front of her suddenly came to life, and again when she heard Hamm's voice.

"Everything's good on my end. The signal should be coming through clearly."

"Yes, it is," Cindy said. "It's not fluctuatin' one little bit."

"Cindy?"

"Yeah, it's the Alabama Bombshell on this end."

"Where's Megan?"

"We switched. She's with Gretchen."

Cindy heard an intake of breath.

"Are you all right, sugar. You didn't have a stroke or nothin', did you?"

•　　　•　　　•

Hamm killed the guidance signal. The last thing he wanted was for the girls to actually find the portal chamber. If they stepped only a few yards into it, they'd be in range of the energy emanations that would set off the antimatter bomb, and he would lose the love of his life.

There was no way to communicate remotely with the girls; Gretchen's highly shielded receptor unit was for one purpose only and he had intentionally not given them any other communication devices, for fear the Zeelons would intercept the signal. He could only hope that when the directional signal died, they would quickly exit via the route by which they had entered the base.

What he had told the girls was true to an extent; the Zeelons were unlikely to harm stray natives, but if the girls were apprehended with the antimatter bomb they would be treated as saboteurs. That would mean the forcible extraction of any memories relating to their mission followed by disintegration in a radiation cubicle.

•   •   •

"What's wrong with this thing?" Gretchen said.

"Huh?" Megan was distracted by faint sounds coming from a downward slanting tunnel in the left wall they had just passed.

"Our directions just blanked out, and I think we still have a bunch more turns to make. What's that?"

"I think it's voices, and they're getting closer."

Gretchen flashed her light around; it lit on a large crack in the smooth wall. "There," she said. "Come on."

Gretchen pushed Megan inside the crack before wedging herself in. The two girls stood jammed against each other face-to-face. Megan was turned away from the mouth of corridor from which the sound was coming, but Gretchen, with a slight tilt of her head, could clearly see a pale light emerge, followed by a vehicle very like Hamm's transport craft except that where his was fan-shaped, this one was long and narrow. It bore two riders standing one behind the other and dressed in close-fitting coveralls. Both were tall and blond, a female in front and a male behind her. Each wore a holster containing a long-barreled sidearm.

"They look just like Hamm," Gretchen whispered.

Megan, with some effort, managed to turn her head enough to see the aliens. "I don't understand," Megan whispered. "They don't look like they'd eat us."

Gretchen took on a feral expression as she eyed the athletic form of the male Zeelon. "Speak for yourself, Princess."

The Zeelons spoke together in a language that sounded vaguely French interspersed with jots of German, like Maurice Chevalier attempting to sing while being repeatedly punched in the gut.

Gretchen saw that the light was emanating from the vehicle, though not from any particular point; the entire thing seemed to glow. She was glad the light was dim and therefore less conducive to their discovery. Even though Hamm had assured the girls that no harm would come to them if they were caught, they did not want to test that. The fact that the aliens were obviously from the same species as Hamm himself was enough to call his veracity into question. He had not outright said they weren't, but he had painted them as monsters.

The aliens stopped talking, and the passage lit up like Times Square on New Years' Eve.

Gretchen shut her eyes and pressed herself back into the crack. She tried mightily to think herself invisible, but when she opened her eyes she found that she was looking into those of the female alien whose craft was now hovering only a few feet away.

Gretchen collected herself and gave Megan an "everything will be fine" look before stepping out from their hiding place.

"My name is Gretchen. This is Megs. We were just out for a hike and found this absolutely lovely cave system to explore. We'll just be going now."

Gretchen took Megan's hand and they began to walk back down the corridor.

The alien craft advanced alongside them for a short distance and then moved ahead and turned crosswise, blocking their further passage.

The female alien said something to her partner and stepped down from the craft. "This is private property," she said, "and you are trespassing."

"Oh, we're sorry," Megan said, "we'll just go."

"Have you gone any deeper into the cave system than this?"

"No," Gretchen said, "we came through the front door and this is as far as we got."

The alien stepped close to Gretchen and took her arm. She looked at the bracelet for a moment and then at the lump in Gretchen's shirt pocket."

"You seem to be carrying something," the alien said. "Let me have it, please."

Gretchen felt sick, but there was nothing she could do except comply. She unbuttoned her shirt pocket, extracted the orb, and handed it over.

"This is not of Earth origin," the Zeelon said, and went to the hovering craft. She showed the orb to her partner and for a while they conferred. Then, leaving the orb with him, she went back to girls.

"You will have to come with us," she said, and gestured toward the craft.

"No, they won't."

The voice was Hamm's. He stood a few yards down the passage and was breathing like he had just finished running a marathon. He held a weapon like the ones the Zeelons carried, and it was pointed at the at the man in the craft.

The woman's right hand moved toward her sidearm, but a look of warning from Hamm stopped its progress. Hamm went first to the transport and took the male Zeelon's weapon out of its holster. He tossed it away and went to the female whom he likewise disarmed.

"We are honored to be in your presence, Your Majesty," the woman said.

"You know my father will never allow this portal to be finished," Hamm said.

The woman shook her head.

"Sabotage, a most dishonorable course," the male Zeelon said.

"I believe you've tried the same thing."

"The unfinished Etherian portal still stands," the woman said. "That should be evidence enough that what you say is false."

"I didn't say you were good at sabotage," Hamm replied, "I only said you engaged in it."

"Wait," Gretchen said to Hamm, "you guys have a portal?"

"Under construction," Hamm said. "It's in the Zagros Mountains. We hope to have it operational soon."

"What?"

"The Zeelons and the Etherians are from the same star system," Hamm explained, "and we are highly competitive. The Emperor has decreed that any planet occupied by inferior civilizations may be claimed for the Empire."

"Wait," Megan said, "you have an Emperor?"

Hamm nodded and continued, "Etheria and Zeelon are both members of the Volian Empire, and both desire the glory of making your planet a colony world."

Gretchen said, "So you wanted us to blow up their thingamadoody so you could conquer Earth first?"

"That's correct."

"You bastard."

"Sticks and stones," Hamm said.

Megan said, "Then all that about your ship's cloaking failing and you getting shot down, none of that was true?"

"There's no such thing as cloaking," Hamm admitted. "I got that from *Star Trek.* I'm a big fan."

"But why us?" Megan asked. "Haven't you got soldiers for this sort of thing?"

"Three tried and failed. I was the fourth, and having no desire to risk my own life, I recruited you."

"I thought you liked me?" Megan said.

"Why do you think I asked you to monitor the signal?"

"Thanks a lot," Gretchen said.

"We have to get out of here," Hamm said. "This section of the base has been shut down since an earthquake comprised its integrity." He gestured to a gaping crack in the wall. "It could collapse unexpectedly."

"Thanks again," Gretchen said.

"That's why I sent you in this way. The Zeelons have largely abandoned it, but, evidently, they still send out occasional patrols. I thought you could make it to the portal chamber before being discovered."

"What good would that have done?" Gretchen asked. "If they caught us, we couldn't plant the bomb."

"About that," Hamm said sheepishly, "it wouldn't have mattered. The antimatter device will explode upon contact with emanations of energy coming from the unfinished portal. You would probably have gotten close enough for, you know — boom."

"You're quite a piece of work, aren't you?" Gretchen said.

Megan said, "It's nice you didn't want me to blow up, but I guess now your plan's a failure."

"Not necessarily," Hamm said.

Hamm handed his weapon to Megan and gave her brief instructions as to how to operate it. Then he ordered the male Zeelon to step down from the craft and relieved him of the orb.

"Remember," he told Megan, "if either of them move, just press the firing stud."

Megan kept her eyes fixed on the Zeelons while darting glances at Hamm who boarded the transport and stood for a moment looking down at the console while his hands played rapidly over the controls. After a moment he hopped down, reclaimed his weapon, and announced, "Everyone head for the entrance, rapidly."

"What did you do?" Gretchen asked accusingly.

"I planted the orb on the transport and set the controls on automatic. It should return to its docking bay."

The female Zeelon gasped. "But that will take it across the portal chamber."

"That's why we should proceed with haste," Hamm said.

When they reached the cave mouth, they found Hamm's ship hovering outside. An obviously concerned Cindy stood, with Oshi beside her, in the entry bay. The little drone made a gesture that looked very much like a thumbs-up and activated the boarding ramp.

"By now, the Zeelons know we're here," Hamm said. "We have to get out before they decide what to do about it."

When the ramp was fully extended, everyone scampered aboard. Hamm escorted the Zeelon prisoners to a cargo hatch and sealed them inside, after which the girls accompanied him to the control room. Hamm took the com while Oshi manned the control panel.

"There are seats against the bulkhead," Hamm said. "I would suggest that you all take one. The ride might be rough."

While looking at a screen full of flickering symbols. Oshi squawked something completely unintelligible to the girls and clearly alarming to Hamm. Hamm replied in the same Franco-German they had heard the Zeelons speak, and the ship rose quickly while simultaneously tilting and veering.

"That was a little rough," Cindy said, straightening up in her seat as the craft leveled.

"It's all right," Hamm replied, "They only fired one missile, and it missed badly."

A short time later, Hamm landed them at the girls' campsite.

"Thank you for your service," he said, as he stood at the foot of the ramp while they debarked.

"Thanks for nothing," Gretchen said. "You were going to kill us."

Cindy looked confused. "What?"

"I'll tell you later," Gretchen said.

Hamm looked contrite. "It is true that I made you unwitting pawns in the rivalry between Etheria and Zeelon. And, in truth, it will make little difference for you which side prevails. As a prize of either, your planet will become a colony world of the Volian Empire and be saved from the terrible fate of conquest by the Tharg Dominion."

"I don't know what that it," Gretchen said, "but it sounds like you're saying you did us a favor."

"And myself. I am the Crown Prince of Etheria. It will be my task and honor to direct the occupation of Earth and someday perhaps usher it into full membership in the Empire. I will not forget your service, and I promise to do all I can to make the transition to galactic awareness as comfortable as possible for your species."

Hamm took a step up the boarding ramp before turning back and looking at Megan.

"Did you forget something?" Megan said.

"No ... yes. That is, I wanted to know if you'd like to see me again. I've grown very fond of you."

Megan looked away. "You mean like go out to dinner, or a movie, or —"

"Something like that."

"Won't you be busy planning the conquest of Earth?"

"Oh, no. I've got people for that."

"Then, okay, I guess. You want my number?"

"While you were aboard my ship your DNA and other bodily markers were scanned and catalogued. I can find you anywhere."

"Just to be sure," Megan said, approaching Hamm with equal parts timidity and coquettishness, "I want to give you something."

Megan reached up and put her arms around Hamm's neck. She pulled his lips to hers and kissed him while she felt the gentle pressure of his arms encircling and holding her.

Megan heard a muffled rumble and thought she felt a vibration under her feet. She looked over her shoulder and saw that the middle peak in the distance was considerably lower, and rounded now instead of triangular.

Hamm let her go and mounted the boarding ramp while Oshi waved goodbye from the top.

A few moments later the ship lifted smoothly and silently into the sky and then streaked off toward the east.

"He's still a bastard," Gretchen said.

"He's my bastard," Megan corrected, "and he's going to be a king.

ABOUT THE AUTHOR

Gary Battershell has published speculative fiction in magazines and anthologies for over twenty years. Since 2019, his output has increased significantly. It includes entries in several anthologies, including *Imps and Minions*, *Bodies*, and *Strangely Funny IX*. Magazine publications include stories in *The Society of Misfit Stories Presents*, *The Fifth Di...*, and *Sci-Fi Lampoon*.

He is currently working on an Edgar Rice Burroughs-style science fiction novel, tentatively titled *Savage World*, and awaiting the publication of stories that include another rom-com (this one set against a Cthulhu Mythos Background); "Deep Love" will be a part of a 2024 two-volume work, *The Necronomi-Romcom* published by Transformations by Obsidian Butterfly.

YOU MIGHT ALSO ENJOY

DENISOVAN HARMONY
by DJ Cockburn

You're watching the first Homo denisova to walk the earth in a hundred and fifty centuries grope their way into adolescence.

LITTLE GREEN MEN
by Curtis Bass

In an orbiting craft, Cooper has a front row seat to the first manned mission to Mars. Their landing is perfect until one crew member claims they are being watched by indigenous creatures.

PARRISH BLUE
by Vanessa MacLaren-Wray

Sallie never expected to discover a world she'd forgotten how to imagine.

Available in digital and trade paperback editions from
Water Dragon Publishing
waterdragonpublishing.com/dragon-gems

www.ingramcontent.com/pod-product-compliance
Lightning Source LLC
Chambersburg PA
CBHW021601310726
48972CB00003B/897